American edition published in 2017 by Andersen Press USA,
an imprint of Andersen Press Ltd.
www.andersenpressusa.com

First published in Great Britain in 2017 by Andersen Press Ltd.,
20 Vauxhall Bridge Road, London SW1V 2SA.

Distributed in the United States and Canada by
Lerner Publishing Group, Inc.
241 First Avenue North
Minneapolis, MN 55401 USA
For reading levels and more information, look up this title at www.lernerbooks.com

Color separated in Switzerland by Photolitho AG, Zürich
Printed and bound in China

Library of Congress Cataloging-in-Publication Data Available
ISBN: 978-1-5124-8127-3
eBook ISBN: 978-1-5124-8151-8
1–TL–7/15/17

OUR KID

Tony Ross

ANDERSEN PRESS USA

Our Kid was late for school again.

He didn't have his homework or his uniform either,
so his teacher sent him straight to the Naughty Corner.

"Please, Sir," squeaked Our Kid.
"I left on time this morning
and my mom said,
'Remember to take
your homework.'

And my dad said, 'Go **straightly** to school,
Our Kid. Don't be late **again.**'

So I **shoffled** my homework into my
bag and took the **shortcut.**

When you take the shortcut
along the beach,
you have to dunkle your
hooves in the water.

Suddenly a submarine **splooshed** up out of the waves and **squeaked** across the sand.

sploosh!

Peeping in a porthole, I saw it was full of water.
And the water was full of fish.

Their leader, Captain Mackerel,
said that they were chasing pirates and
could take me to school on the way.

As it was too watery inside the submarine, I rode on the deck, and off we bumpeeded down the road. But before the fish could find the pirates…

... the pirates found the fish!
These were dinopirates, so some were
squiddly, but others were felumpingly big.

The big ones shook the
submarine.

The fish were safe inside, but I fell into the pirates' clutches.

They **snitched** my pants and my schoolbag.

"My homework's in that!" I cried, as the pirates **sniggled** and bounded away.

I tried to **stop** them, but they were too big.
And if I had, they probably would've **eaten** me.

"Hello!" **boomdered** a voice.

An elephant had snuck up behind me. He was **not** a wild elephant, because he was wearing a belt and a **shed** on his back.

He asked me, 'Why so **glumbumtious**, little goat?'

I told him how late I was for school, so he
offered me a lift, high up on his back.

Which was lucky, because it was a long way over the **craggly** mountains and across the **wide** blue water. And I got to see it all, without getting **snarked** by crocodiles.

When we got to school, I said thank you and the elephant **kerlumped** away.

And that's why I got here **so** late, **without** my homework or my pants."

"Our Kid, be hushled!" cried the teacher.

"Children, what do we call someone who makes up such total and utter nonsense?"

A good goat is on time, does their homework, and never lies.

But just then...

Kerumble!

The school began to shake. Desks tipped over and chairs bounced around as everybody scrambled out of the nearest window or door.

But **Our Kid** wasn't allowed to leave the Naughty Corner... so he was still there when **three** aliens walked in!

The **dinopirate** was excited to be visiting a new planet, and the whole class waved good-bye as the spaceship zerumbled off.

Then everyone ran back inside.

"You were bravey to face the aliens like that," said his teacher.

Our Kid handed in his homework, and the teacher gave him a gold star and an apple, without even reading it.

"You can be as late as you like tomorrow," he chuckled.

This time Our Kid skipped straight home,
with no shortcuts and his head full of adventures.

"You're back early," said his mom.
"So, what happened today?" asked his dad.

"Nuffin," said Our Kid.